W9-CAS-174

Diana, Maybe

Crescent Dragonwagon
illustrations by Deborah Kogan Ray

Macmillan Publishing Company   New York

Text copyright © 1987 by Crescent Dragonwagon
Illustrations copyright © 1987 by Deborah Kogan Ray
All rights reserved. No part of this book may be reproduced or
transmitted in any form or by any means, electronic or mechanical,
including photocopying, recording, or by any information storage and
retrieval system, without permission in writing from the Publisher.
The lines from the song "Hey, Good Lookin' " by Hank Williams
(© Copyright 1979 Acuff-Rose/Opryland Music, Inc., and Hiriam
Music, Inc. International copyright secured. All rights reserved.)
appear by permission of the publishers.
Macmillan Publishing Company
866 Third Avenue, New York, NY 10022
Collier Macmillan Canada, Inc.
First Edition
Printed in the United States of America

10 9 8 7 6 5 4 3 2 1

The text of this book is set in 14 point ITC Zapf International Light.
The illustrations are rendered in pencil.
Library of Congress Cataloging-in-Publication Data
Dragonwagon, Crescent. Diana, maybe.
Summary: Rosie speculates about what her life would
be like if she ever met her half sister, Diana.
[1. Sisters—Fiction. 2. Divorce—Fiction]
I. Ray, Deborah Kogan, ill. II. Title.
PZ7.D7824Di 1987   [E]   86-12432
ISBN 0-02-733180-6

For Lyn Littlefield Hoopes
half sister found
Love, Crescent

For Hilda
D.K.R.

On Sunday mornings,
when my father stands at the stove
wearing his blue bathrobe
and flipping over the blueberry pancakes,
he sings a song that goes
"Hey, good-lookin',
what you got cookin'?"
while my mother,
in a red caftan,
squeezes the oranges
for juice and sings along.
As I put out the syrup and butter
and the special Sunday-morning plates
with the flowers at the edge
for my mother and father and me,
I wish I could put out another plate,
for Diana.

I have a half sister named Diana.
I've never met her,
but I think about her.
I wonder what she's like,
and if I'd like her,
and if she'd like me.
I know her name,
and that she has brown eyes.
I know that a long time before
my father met my mother,
before they loved each other,
before they got married,
before they had me,
my daddy was married to another woman,
and they had Diana,
in another city faraway
where it rains a lot.
"Another life," says my father. "And
I didn't live it well."
He always looks sad
when he says it.

I hear my father singing as he cooks the pancakes,
and I remember his saying, "It was another life,"
and sometimes I think,
How could there have been any life but this
for my father? How could he have been married
to someone else, and have another little girl?
But there was,
and he did,
and Diana, my half sister, is living somewhere now,
and even though
she was only three months old
when her mother and my father divorced,
she must think about my father now
because he is her father, too.
She must wonder what he's like,
maybe the way I wonder what she's like.

I wonder if
in that rainy city Diana lives in,
with her mother and stepfather,
she is having pancakes for breakfast
right now.
"I don't know," says my father,
"I don't know."
When I ask him, he looks sad,
as he always does
when he talks about Diana.

I wonder if she even knows about me.
"I don't know, Rosie-pumpkin," says my father.
"I don't know what her mother has told her
about me and my life now.
Her mother was very angry with me
when we divorced,
and she had many good reasons to be."

Diana is six years older than me.
Sometimes
when my parents are downstairs talking
and I'm upstairs alone in bed
but not asleep,
I imagine that Diana is my real sister,
living here with us.
She would be right in this room, in the other bed,
and we could talk in the dark.
At the end of school,
when I found out who my next year's teacher would be,
she could say, "Oh, Mr. Parkin? I had him. He's not bad."

I could tell her
things I don't tell anyone ...
like that I can't blow bubbles out of bubble gum,
and that when I try to snap my fingers
I don't make any sound,
and that I don't get a note
when I blow across the top of a Coke bottle.
She'd say, "Here, it's easy, you just do this—"
and she'd show me how,
and I'd be able to do it.

Sometimes she'd braid my hair for me
with a long purple ribbon
braided into it, all the way down,
and a big bow at the end.
Sometimes she'd let me brush her hair.
Maybe she wears it short,
but I always picture it long and brown,
like mine.
"Isn't it amazing," people would say,
"how much those two sisters look alike
and how well they get along?"

I'd tell Diana riddles I heard at school.

"Diana, when did the farmer hurt his corn?"

"I don't know, Rosie. When?"

"When he pulled its ears."

"Oh, no! Why do they have such awful jokes
  in the second grade?"

"They're not awful, Diana. They're *funny!*
  Want to hear another one?"

"No, I certainly don't," she'd say, but I'd tell her anyway.

"Diana, why don't bears need shoes?"

"I give up. Why?"

"Because they've got *bear feet!*"

"Oh, no! No more, Rosie. These are *awful!*"

But she'd be laughing, and she wouldn't really mean it.
And sometimes she'd tell me a joke.

"Rosie, there was this man who went into a store and he
said to the lady behind the counter, 'I'd like a pound of
kidley beans, please.' And she said, 'I'm sorry, sir, we don't
have kidley beans. Perhaps you mean *kidney* beans?' And
he got very mad at her and said, 'I said *kidley*, diddle I?'"
Diana and I would laugh and laugh.

Sometimes we'd go shopping together in the mall
with my mother.
If I wanted an orange sweatshirt and socks
and my mother said, "Absolutely not. It's just *too* orange,"
and she wouldn't listen to me, Diana could say,
"But, Mom, everyone at school is wearing at least one piece
of neon Day-Glo clothing this year. You've just got to let her,"
and maybe my mother would.

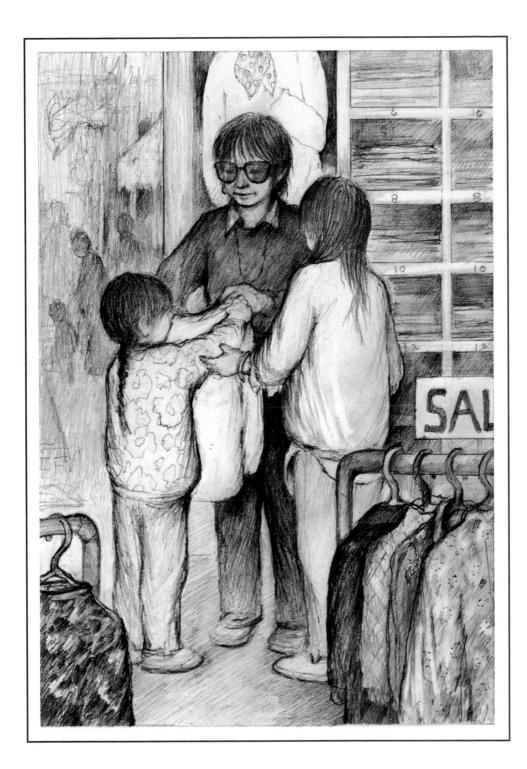

And maybe Diana would get herself a neon sweatshirt, too, in green.

And maybe she'd let me borrow it sometimes.

"But, Rosie," Diana would say, "it'll be way too big for you."

"I could belt it," I'd say.

"If I lend it to you," she'd say, "will you *promise* to be very, very, very careful and not spill anything on it?"

"I promise, cross my heart and hope to die."

"Well, okay, if you're really very careful and you promise, you can borrow it, but just this once."

And I would be very careful
and all day I'd feel good at school
because I was wearing
a beautiful big green sweatshirt
that belonged to my big sister.
My sister.

But Diana is only my half sister,
and she lives far away
with her mother and her new father.
I've never met her
and she may not even know about me.
And it's sad.
But maybe someday it won't be.
Maybe someday her mother
will let her visit us,
and maybe Diana
will like it so much
she'll stay with us forever.

Or maybe we could at least be pen pals.
Or maybe we can meet when we're grown up,
and camp out together,
or fly airplanes,
or visit the Eiffel Tower in Paris, France,
or write a book together,
about two faraway sisters
who find each other.

I hope Diana *does* know about me.
I hope she thinks about me, though we've never met.
I hope she thinks, "I wonder
what my half sister, Rosie, is like.
I wonder what she's doing
right now."
I hope that maybe Diana knows
that what I'm doing now
is thinking of her.